PET Peeves of Flying

PET Peeves of Flying

Emily J. Barnett

Allen Press

PET Peeves of Flying

Published by Allen Press

For further information, please contact:
Allen Press
Jean Barnett
P.O. Box 680155, Marietta, Georgia 30068
petpeevesoftheanimalworld.com
petpeeves@bellsouth.net

Book design by:
ARBOR BOOKS, INC.
19 Spear Road, Ste 202
Ramsey, NJ 07446
www.arborbooks.com

Printed in the United States

Library of Congress Control Number: 2006902010
ISBN: 0-9778770-0-0

Acknowledgements

I would like to dedicate this book to my mother, who planted the seed that grew into this dream of wild imagination and fantasy. I would also like to acknowledge the positive influence and inspiration that I received from my long time and loyal friend, Sheba, a beautiful Labrador/Greyhound mix who gave me the idea for my animal characters. Neither is here today to realize how much they contributed to this project, but they will always live in my heart and influence my work.

This book could not have been written without the support and encouragement of my family. They gave me hope and strength when I thought I had none left. They gave me a reason to continue when I couldn't find one. They were my rock.

I'd like to give a special thanks to the Delta and United Airline flight attendants, pilots, and customer service representatives. Some thought I was writing up complaints about them as I probed for information to use in my book. But as we talked more and more, many began to realize what this was all about and were very excited to talk about their adventures in flying. Every situation presented a unique and entertaining story.

In addition, I would like to thank my fellow passengers for their feedback on airline procedures and in-flight experiences. They were truly the ones who contributed the most to the situations depicted in this book. Though most people do not enjoy being made fun of, or being the brunt of a joke, many were more than willing to allow me to use their personal experiences.

A very special thank you goes out to my niece, Ashlee Monet Craver, who did all of the creative illustrations for this book. Ashlee and I were a team. I would give her the scenario, and not only would she draw the animal doing what he would normally do in that situation, but she would also choose the appropriate animal for that particular scene. We had incredible chemistry. Ashlee, thank you so much for your uncanny insight and enormous talents.

And last, but certainly not least, I would like to thank God; none of this would be possible without his blessings. When things were not happening when and how I wanted them to, I wondered if God wanted this for me. I prayed that he would show me signs if I should proceed. Though it was not always an easy task, he showed me how to do it. Though I constantly questioned if it was in the plan, he assured me it was. Even when it seemed that the cost would be more than I could afford, he gave me the okay to "just do it." Thank you, God, for believing in me.

Introduction

Airline travel has become quite complicated, with going through security, having too much luggage, the type of food we eat (if we are fortunate enough to get food), and of course, trying to navigate the various airports.

Imagine walking headlong into a stampede of people who are charging like bulls at the gate. That is what it can be like when boarding an airplane. Then once you're on the plane, imagine how the crew would react to the many different characteristics and requirements of their passengers, who do everything from floss their teeth on board to raid the plane of its amenities.

Flight #826 is about to take off with many such characters on board. You might even refer to them as animals as they display their odd and often rude and insensitive behaviors. Please come on board as we begin one of the most interesting voyages of all time. Picture yourself flying with many different species of the animal kingdom, from kangaroos to elephants. How will they interact with each other as they attempt to reach their destination? How will the crew handle their needs as they, too, try to reach their destination with full faculties intact?

Sit back, buckle your seat belts, and prepare for takeoff. Flight #826 is now departing.

Boarding

"I'm sorry Mr. Camel, you have excess baggage.
There is an extra fee."

"Okay, I'll carry this one on board."

"Mrs. Roo, I will have to check your pouch."

"I must remove these scissors, Mrs. Roo.
No sharp objects are allowed on board the aircraft."

Why are there always passengers who want to crowd my counter?

"Please stand back until you are called for boarding."

BOARDING

"Are you boarding yet?"

BOARDING

"Mrs. Fox, you are only allowed
one piece of luggage and one personal item,
such as a purse or a laptop computer."

"You've crammed it, but if it fits, that's fine!"

"Mr. Gibbons, do you have your boarding card?"

"Out of my way! Here's my ticket,
am I going to make the flight?"

"To help the boarding process,
when you find your seat,
please step out of the aisle
to let others pass."

"Do you have any seats
with a bit more room?"

"Is this better, Mr. Ralph?"

"Mrs. Wombat, you may only have one pouch baby.
The larger one must occupy a seat."

Some passengers must think they are kings.
Why doesn't anyone close the bin
after stowing their luggage?

"I need someone to put away my luggage."

"Mrs. Feline, I'll assist you in finding a space, but you will need to put away your own luggage."

"Mr. Possum, are you okay?"

"He has a pulse.
I think he is afraid of sitting next to Mr. Lionson.
Perhaps we can get someone to switch
seats with Mr. Possum."

"Ugh! There's a disgusting fly.
Even Mr. Skunk is repelled by him."

"We can't take off with Mr. Fly on board. I will have to get a customer service representative to remove him."

"I'll offer Mr. Cheetah a beverage
when he gets off the phone.
He's talking a mile a minute."

"Hey! You missed me!! I want a drink!!"

"Passengers sitting in the emergency exit rows must be able to open the exits and assist passengers on the way out."

"I want to remain in this seat.
I can lift twenty times my weight and
I can assist others out of the exit."

"May I please have your attention for the safety demonstration?"

"Mr. and Mrs. Hyena, you must keep
the laughing down until after
the safety announcement."

In-flight

"I can't get the door open. Can you help me?"

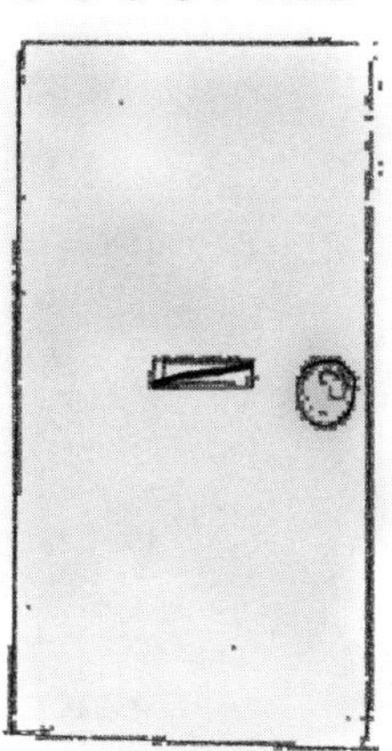

"The sign says 'occupied.'
See the line? Someone is in the toilet."

"Oh my stars!!!"
EEK!

"Kitty, you must keep your pet
in its container during the flight."

"Excuse me, Mr. Bull.
Please get your hooves off the tray table!"

I can't believe he did that. We serve food on these tray tables. The "hide" of some passengers!

"I'll just have coffee, black."

She asked for black coffee
and she has rung her bell twice—
first for sugar, then for cream.
Why didn't she just say,
"Coffee, cream and sugar"?

Hmmmm...peanuts.
I'll just help myself

"Mr. Phant, I'll be with you in a moment.
Please don't help yourself."

I don't believe he is yanking on my dress!
SNAG SNAG

"Mr Gazelle! In the future, I strongly suggest using your call bell if you would like a beverage or are in need of assistance."

"I'll have another, honey! Make it a double."

"Mr. Fish, I can give you coffee or a soft drink, but I can't serve you any more alcohol."

"Miss!! Miss!! Hop to it!"

"Mr. Frog had the nerve to snap his fingers at me. I'm not going near him. Someone else will have to serve that 'toad.'"

"Sir! Sir!! Sir!!!

"I'll take it!"

"I can't eat this meal. This is not what I ordered."

"I'm sorry, Mr. Aardvark, we are all out of ants."

"May I have a Coke?"

"Here's your Coke!" "Here's your Coke!"
"Mr. Pelia, Please don't order
from every attendant!"

"Good grief!!"

"We're serving food.
Why doesn't Mr. Skunk realize he
should close the door afterwards!"

"What would you like to drink?"

How much longer must I wait?

"Here! Can you take this?"

I don't believe this.
Couldn't he wait
for the cart!

"Miss! Could you help me?"

That was inconsiderate and gross.
"Mr. Walrus, here is a glass of water, and the bathroom will give you privacy!"

"We have Coke, Sprite, orange juice,
tomato juice, diet drinks, water, beer,
cocktails, coffee, tea and wine."

"Huh!? What do you have to drink?"

Can't anyone control those kids?

"You kids will have to
stop kicking the seats in front of you."

"It's Mr. Sloth! He's asleep."

"Excuse me!
Mr. Sloth, you're leaning on the call bell!"

Oh No!!

"Mrs. Swine, if you will put your
dirty diaper in this bag, I'll dispose of it."

"Here are your headsets."

"Oh, I am so sorry.
I didn't realize my foot was in the aisle."

"Here is your Coke, Piney."

My first thank you.
Music to my ears!!

"I'm cold. Could you warm up the plane?"

The plane is fine.
She needs clothes!

"Ms. Dolphina, you will have
to fasten your seat belt."

I can't believe no one has
their seat belts on
in this turbulence

"What's going on? He's cutting the line!!"

"Mr. Asp, there is a line.
You cannot slither to the front."

"Mrs. Catrina, the cart
is coming and your kitty is in the aisle."

"Can I get you something to drink?"

"Help! I can't get this door open!"

"Mr. Don Key, perhaps you
should use the knob and not the ashtray."

"Do you have anything for my kids to play with?"

"I have some things.
Since the airlines have had to
really cut back, I bring my own."

"I'd like a-a-a..."

I can't believe he just did that!

SODA
Chips

Where does all this trash come from?

"Oh! So that's what you do behind the curtain."

"The airport has been shut down due to weather.
There is no landing or taking off."

Will I make my connection?
Every time I take this airline, there's a problem.
How long will this last?

Deplaning

"Please remain seated until the aircraft comes to a complete stop and the seatbelt sign has been turned off."

I can make it to the front
before anyone gets up.

No one will miss
any of this.
SNAG
Fly

He thinks we're stupid.
"Good-bye! Thanks for flying with us."

"Thank you for flying with us, Mr. Crabb."

"That was the worst landing
ever and the flight was terrible.
I've seen all the movies,
and the food was awful."

"Who knows, you may be in this seat someday."